Holiday Histories

Flag Day

Mir Tamim Ansary

Heinemann Library
Chicago, Illinois

© 2002, 2006 Heinemann Library
an imprint of Capstone Global LLC.
Chicago, Illinois

Customer Service 888-454-2279
Visit our website at www.heinemannraintree.com

Designed by Kimberly Miracle and Q2A Creative
Printed in the United States of America in Stevens Point, Wisconsin.

082011
006335RP

New edition ISBNs: 1-4034-8886-X (hardcover)
                            1-4034-8899-1 (paperback)

The Library of Congress has cataloged the first edition as follows:
Ansary, Mir Tamim.
    Flag Day / Mir Tamim Ansary.
        p. cm. -- (Holiday histories)
    Includes bibliographical references and index.
    ISBN 1-58810-222-X (lib. bdg.)
    1. Flag Day – Juvenile literature. [1. Flag Day. 2. Flags – United States – History. 3. Holidays] I. Title.

JK1761 .A57 2001
394.263 – dc21
                            2001000072

Acknowledgments
The author and publishers are grateful to the following for permission to reproduce photographs: The Bridgeman Art Library p. 15 (Historical Society of Pennsylvania); Corbis pp. 4-5 (Zefa), 9 (Reuters), 12, 16, 22, 29; Culver Pictures p. 25; Getty p. 18 (FPG); The Granger Collection pp. 7, 10, 11, 17, 27, 28; North Wind Pictures pp. 8, 14, 19, 20-21; Photo Edit p. 6 (Gary Conner); SuperStock p. 13; Underwood Photo Archives pp. 23, 24, 26.

Cover photograph reproduced with permission of Photodisc/Getty Images.

Every effort has been made to contact copyright holders of any material reproduced in this book. Any omissions will be rectified in subsequent printings if notice is given to the publisher.

Disclaimer
All the Internet addresses (URLs) given in this book were valid at the time of going to press. However, due to the dynamic nature of the Internet, some addresses may have changed, or sites may have changed or ceased to exist since publication. While the author and publisher regret any inconvenience this may cause readers, no responsibility for any such changes can be accepted by either the author or the publisher.

Contents

Some words are shown in bold, **like this**. You can find out what they mean by looking in the glossary.

Flag Day

June 14 may seem like just another day.
Summer vacation is now a few weeks old.
Most adults have gone to work.

But look around your neighborhood. You may
see more flags than usual. That is because
June 14 is not just another day. It is Flag Day.

A Promise of Loyalty

On this day, our country's flag is flown from many buildings. It is **honored** in our nation's **capital**. People gather to say the Pledge of Allegiance.

People show their loyalty to our country by flying flags during elections, Fourth of July celebrations, and Flag Day.

In the Pledge of Allegiance, people promise their **loyalty** to the flag. But they are not just talking about a piece of cloth. The flag is much more than that.

How Flags Were Invented

Flags were invented for use in war. Leaders held them up on crowded battlefields. Then soldiers could see where their leader was.

A leader's flag came to stand for the leader.
Then it came to stand for the leader's land
and people. By the 1600s, every country had
its own special flag.

Our First Flags

Our country formed after we won a war. We started as thirteen **colonies** controlled by **Great Britain**. We went to war to become a country of our own.

Grand Union Flag or Continental Colors, 1775–1777

DONT TREAD ON ME

Continental Navy Flag, 1776

The **colonists** had several flags at first. One looked like the British flag. Another showed a snake over the words "Don't **tread** on me."

The Stars and Stripes

A man named Francis Hopkinson **designed** a new flag. It had thirteen stars and stripes, one for each **colony**. On June 14, 1777, the **colonists** chose this flag.

Francis Hopkinson

After the war, the colonists formed a new country.
But they kept the "Stars and Stripes" as their flag.
Each star and each stripe now stood for a state.

Changing Country, Changing Flag

But the new country was still growing. Its people were moving west. The **government** was buying or getting more land.

This picture shows a Fourth of July celebration in 1818. Our country had twenty states then.

New states kept forming. The flag had to be changed with each new state. One more star and stripe had to be added.

Back to Thirteen Stripes

By 1818 our country had twenty states. With twenty stripes, the flag looked too crowded. American leaders agreed to one last change.

They decided the flag would always have just thirteen stripes. These would stand for the first thirteen **colonies**. Only a star was added for each new state after that.

The First Flag Day

In 1885 the flag was 108 years old. That year a teacher in Wisconsin named Bernard Cigrand had an idea. He and his students held a birthday party for the flag.

George Balch's kindergarten class would have looked like this one from the 1880s.

Another teacher named George Balch taught kindergarten in New York City. He also had his students celebrate Flag Day.

The Flag Day Celebration

On those early Flag Days, students gathered at their schools. Each student was given a small flag.

Then they sang **patriotic** songs. They listened to speeches about their country. They **saluted** the flag as it was raised.

Flag Day Spreads

Balch told the leaders of the New York schools about his flag party. They were in charge of all the schools in New York. They liked what Balch had done.

They asked that all New York schools **observe** Flag Day in 1889. The idea soon spread. In Chicago, 300 thousand children took part in Flag Day in 1894.

Schools outside of New York also celebrated Flag Day.

Flag Day in World War One

In 1916 a **world war** was being fought. Our country was about to join in. President Woodrow Wilson wanted the country to feel **patriotic**.

He called for a **national** Flag Day that year. The flag was **honored** across the country. After the war, people continued to celebrate Flag Day.

Flag Day Becomes Official

By 1949 another **world war** had ended. Our soldiers had helped to win this war. Americans felt proud.

These soldiers celebrate the end of World War Two. It lasted from 1939 to 1945.

Harry Truman

President Harry Truman signed a law that said Flag Day should be celebrated every year. Today it is **observed** in every state. In Pennsylvania it is a holiday.

War and Peace

Many people think of soldiers when they see the flag. Soldiers have carried our flag into many battles. But the flag is not just about war.

Explorers, athletes, artists, and scientists have also carried our flag. On Flag Day, we **honor** our country's strength in peace as well as in war.

Important Dates

Flag Day

1775	The **colonists** begin their war for independence
1777	Americans choose the Stars and Stripes as their flag
1783	The United States becomes a country
1818	Congress changes the flag back to having thirteen stripes
1877	The flag is one hundred years old
1885	Flag Day is celebrated by Bernard Cigrand and his class
1889	Flag Day is **observed** by the New York schools
1894	300 thousand children celebrate Flag Day in Chicago
1916	President Wilson **declares** a **national** Flag Day
1949	President Truman declares a yearly Flag Day
1960	The last two stars are added to the United States flag

Glossary

capital   important city where the government of a country or state is based

colony   land owned or controlled by another country

colonists   people who live in a colony

declare   state something

design   think, draw, or build something new

government   people in charge of a country

Great Britain   name that includes England, Scotland, and Wales. People from Great Britain are called British.

honor   show respect for someone or something

loyalty   being faithful to; on the side of

national   having to do with the whole nation

observe   celebrate

patriotic   showing love of one's country

saluted   greeted with respect

tread   step or walk on

world war   war in which many nations fight

Find Out More

Binns, Tristan Boyer. *The American Flag*. Chicago: Heinemann Library, 2001.

Schaefer, Lola. *The Pledge of Allegiance*. Chicago: Heinemann Library, 2002.

Schuh, Mari C. *Flag Day*. Mankato, Minn.: Capstone, 2003.

Index